EAGLES

EAGLES
Joe Van Wormer

Lodestar Books E. P. Dutton New York

The photographs in this book were taken by the author
except as follows:
    The photographs on pages 23, 25, 26, and 35
    are by Michael W. Collopy.
    The left photograph on page 46 is by
    Frank Isaacs.

Library of Congress Cataloging in Publication Data

Van Wormer, Joe.
    Eagles.

    "Lodestar books."
    Summary: Describes the physical characteristics,
habits, and behavior of two species of eagles:
the American or bald eagle and the golden eagle.
    1. Bald eagle—Juvenile literature.   2. Golden
eagle—Juvenile literature.   [1. Bald eagle.   2. Golden
eagle.   3. Eagles]   I. Title.
QL696.F32V36   1985   598'.916   84-13684
ISBN 0-525-67154-4

Published in the United States by E. P. Dutton, Inc.,
2 Park Avenue, New York, N.Y. 10016

Published simultaneously in Canada by
Fitzhenry & Whiteside Limited, Toronto

Editor: Virginia Buckley   Designer: Suzanne Haldane

Printed in the U.S.A.   W   First Edition
10 9 8 7 6 5 4 3 2

to wildlife researchers, biologists, and
students, whose unceasing efforts continue to
add to man's knowledge of the wonders of
the natural world around us

There are two species of eagles in North America: the American or bald eagle, *Haliaeetus leucocephalus*, found only on this continent; and the golden eagle, *Aquila chrysaëtos*, which also lives in Europe, Asia, and North Africa. Males and females of each species look the same. They have a wingspan of 6½ to 8 feet. Females weigh up to 14 pounds; males are smaller, weighing 8 to 10 pounds. Bald eagles are slightly larger, up to 36 inches in length.

Not too much is known about the life span of an eagle in the wild, but it is thought to be about thirty years. Captive eagles have lived for about fifty years.

Mature birds are easily recognized. The bald eagle has a snow-white head and tail, along with a bright yellow beak, yellow eyes, and yellow feet. Its body is brownish black. This eagle was named in the seventeenth century, apparently by early English settlers, who derived the word *bald* from the English and Welsh *balde*, which meant white.

1

The golden eagle is dark brown with dark brown eyes. Golden or light brown feathers on the back of the neck and the top of the head give this eagle its name. The golden eagle's beak and claws are black, and its legs and feet are feathered all the way down to its yellow toes.

The young golden eagle shows some white under its wings and has a white tail with a broad black band at the tip.

3

The bald eagle's legs and feet are not feathered all the way down. It is this difference that distinguishes the young bald eagle, which is mostly dark brown with brownish bill and eyes, from the golden eagle. The bald eagle's head, tail, beak, and eyes whiten a little each year until, at age four or five, they attain the full dramatic adult coloration.

Eagles are splendid fliers, leisurely flapping their massive wings or simply soaring—seemingly motionless—on updrafts of warm air at from 28 to 44 miles per hour. Golden eagles may keep this up for hours, rising in great spirals until they are mere specks in the sky. Then, spotting their prey with eyes of remarkable resolving power—about eight times finer than human eyes—they fold their wings and drop toward their prey at estimated speeds of 150 to 200 miles per hour.

5

While the flight of the bald eagle is powerful, it is more labored and less graceful than that of the golden eagle. However, in pursuit of prey such as waterfowl, the bald eagle, too, is fast and deadly.

7

Birds that spend as much time in the air as eagles do take good care of their all-important feathers. Ordinarily, after feeding, an eagle will settle on a favorite perch and begin cleaning and combing its feathers. This is called preening. It is a big job as adults have over seven thousand feathers. Young birds start preening as soon as their feathers begin to appear.

Eagles, like this immature bald eagle, also bathe frequently along the edges of streams or in any standing water that is available.

All birds molt, or lose feathers, at least once a year and then grow new ones that replace worn and faded plumage. Eagles do not lose all their large wing-feathers in a single annual molt, so they maintain flying ability.

Eagles, like other birds, have three eyelids: two that work up and down, and a third—closer to the eye—called the nictitating membrane. This third eyelid flicks sideways across the eye every few seconds, cleaning and moistening the cornea. Since it is transparent, the membrane does not block the bird's vision.

Eagles also have excellent hearing, although their ears, located on each side of the head, are not used for hunting. But any little noise instantly alerts them.

An eagle's feet—with their long, needle-sharp, curved talons—are its hunting and attack weapons. Actually, what we call feet are really the bird's toes. It stands with its toes on the ground and its heels in the air. When resting its feet, the eagle folds its claws. The toes, when spread, may cover an area as large as a man's hand and have enough strength to pierce and kill medium-sized mammals and birds.

11

The wicked-looking hooked beak is also quite strong and acts as both hand and mouth. With it, the bird holds and carries nesting material. The beak can tear, cut, or crush, depending on what is being eaten. The beak is covered with a hard, horny material that continually renews itself toward the tip.

12

Despite its fierce look, great size, and powerful flying ability, the eagle does not have a voice to match its appearance. The scream of the bald eagle is more like a squeaky squeal. The golden eagle is generally silent. Its sound has been described as a *kee-kee-kee*, or it may give a high-pitched scream or squeal.

Nevertheless, eagles are majestic creatures whose piercing eyes look out at the world from proud and stern features, unafraid even of their only enemy—man. It is a memorable experience to see an eagle close up for the first time.

The eagle's magnificence has influenced people since the Old Stone Age, when drawings of this great bird first appeared in European caves. Many European and Asian cultures have used the eagle to symbolize power, courage, freedom, independence, truth, and immortality. During the period when falconry flourished in Europe, only kings and emperors were permitted to fly the mighty golden eagle, often called the king of birds.

Eagles were also revered by various American Indian tribes. Feathers, wooden images of eagles, and stuffed skins were used to confer honor on worthy warriors and as decorations in council lodges. The Indians believed that eagle feathers brought swiftness, strength, and endurance to their wearers. (Although it is now illegal to have feathers unless owned prior to passage of eagle protection laws, Indians are allowed to receive feathers from the Department of the Interior.)

After the war in which the United States won its independence from England, this country adopted the American bald eagle as the principal figure in its Great Seal. Since then, the bald eagle has been constantly with us. It is on the back of every one-dollar bill. It has been used extensively on coins since the early eighteenth century and is currently on twenty-five and fifty cent pieces.

Since 1851, twenty-seven different U.S. postage stamps have featured this bird. Nearly every state has eagle place-names, and the bird is included in the state seals of Pennsylvania, Mississippi, Illinois, Missouri, Arkansas, Michigan, Iowa, Oregon, Utah, New Mexico, Wyoming, and also the District of Columbia.

This national symbol is seen on the top of flagpoles and as ornaments on bridges, public buildings, and memorial structures. It is on naval uniform insignia, and Eagle Scout is the highest rank in the Boy Scouts of America. Above is an eagle over the window at the Denver, Colorado, mint. The mosaic, right, is on the floor of the mint.

The name *eagle* has been given to commercial products varying from condensed milk to motorcars. There are various eagle athletic teams, and there is a Fraternal Order of Eagles.

When astronaut Neil A. Armstrong announced from the moon the fact of man's first landing there, he reported, "The Eagle has landed!" *Eagle* was the name given to the first lunar module.

19

Despite the almost overwhelming presence of eagle images and names, most Americans have never seen one in the wild.

Eagles nest in high, remote places that are often inaccessible. Bald eagles mostly nest in trees, but will occasionally choose a rocky ledge if a suitable tree is not available. The preferred nesting sites of golden eagles are rocky cliffs above good hunting grounds in mountainous areas. When such sites are not available, they will build in a suitable tree.

21

It is believed that eagles mate for life when they become adults at around four and a half to five years of age. If something happens to one of the pair, the survivor will find another mate. Courtship displays during the late winter breeding season consist mostly of spectacular flying exhibitions at high speed, along with various intricate aerial maneuvers. In the bald eagles' amazing cartwheel display, the two eagles swoop at each other, avoiding collisions with side slips and fast climbs. One bird turns on its back and locks talons with the other. Thus tied together, they fall toward the earth, spinning like a cartwheel. A few feet above the ground, they release each other and zoom back into the air.

Nests are constructed mostly of sticks that may be as much as 2 inches in diameter and up to 6 feet long. The nest cavity in the center, where the eggs will be laid, is hollowed out and finished with a soft lining of moss, feathers, fur, and lichen. Nest materials are usually carried in the bird's talons, but are placed into position with the beak. Nest building and repairing continues during incubation and while the eaglets remain at the nest. Strange things have been found as parts of eagles' nests—broomsticks, lumber, a tablecloth, even bones of large mammals.

Choice nesting sites are used year after year. One bald eagle's nest was occupied continuously for over thirty-four years. Each nesting season, a new nest is built on top of the old. After several years, this layered nest becomes very large—7 to 8 feet across and as much as 12 feet deep.

One bald eagle's nest in Florida was 20 feet deep and 9½ feet across. Another contained an estimated 4,000 pounds of nesting material. However, nests on cliffs are never as large, because they don't have the framework of tree branches to support them.

23

Both golden and bald eagles may have several nesting sites in their chosen area and use them on alternate years. Various small bird species often build their nests in the lower parts of these large eagle nests, and thus are protected from attacks by other predatory birds.

Egg laying starts early in the southern parts of the eagle's range. The further north an eagle lives, the later it lays its eggs. Southern bald eagles may lay as early as November, while those furthest north may not lay until June.

In North America, the golden eagle is found mostly from Alaska through the plains regions of the West and into Mexico. There are a few in eastern Canada, the Great Lakes states, and the Appalachian Mountains of the East. Those in the southern areas may start laying as early as February and, in the northern parts, as late as June.

Eagles usually lay two eggs, which are quite small in comparison to the size of the bird. The bald eagle's eggs are a dull white; the golden's are splotched with brown. A chicken egg, seen in the center of the photograph, is smaller than either.

For golden eagles, incubation requires forty-three to forty-five days. The female does most of the incubating, while the male supplies the food. The female may be nervous on the nest, fuss with the eggs, rearrange nest materials, and preen. Or she may sit quietly, occasionally walking around the nest and stretching her legs and wings—just to relax.

The incubation period for bald eagles has been reported to be thirty-four to thirty-five days. Bald eagles seem to share the incubating chores more evenly, and each parent takes care of its own food needs. If the eggs are left for even a short length of time, they are carefully covered with grass, stubble, and any other fine nesting material that is available. When the parent bird returns, the uncovering process may take from five to ten minutes.

Females usually help the eaglets chip off their eggshells, then the females carry the shells away from the nest. The newly hatched golden eaglet is covered with gray-tipped white down, which is replaced in a few days with creamy white down of a thicker texture. The initial downy covering of the just-hatched bald eaglet is a thick, silky, light gray—with a touch of darker gray in spots. The eaglet's head, chin, and underparts are white. The bill and eyes are dark. In about three weeks, the bird gets a second, thicker and darker, gray coat of down. At five to six weeks, contour feathers begin to appear. Two weeks later, the eaglet is well feathered.

When hatched, the eaglets, which weigh between 3 and 4 ounces, have disproportionately large heads and are completely helpless. They bear little resemblance to the handsome adult birds they will become.

Both parent bald eagles bring food to the nest. However, the male golden eagle is the main provider for his young. Small mammals will already be skinned; birds will be plucked. The female does most of the feeding. She holds the prey with her feet and rips off pieces small enough for the young birds to swallow. She offers them bits of food in her beak. At first the youngsters have trouble grasping these offerings, but in a few days they become quite skillful at it. The female may help herself to a bite once in a while, but the male feeds away from the nest.

Because the eggs are laid several days apart and incubation starts as soon as the eggs are laid, one eaglet hatches sooner and is older and larger than the other. Immediately it begins to take advantage of the smaller one. This may consist of pecking with its sharp beak and preventing the weaker one from getting its share of food. As a result, the smaller bird is often killed by its stronger nest mate, or it may simply starve to death. Oddly enough, the parents appear to be unaware of the younger bird's mistreatment and do nothing to stop it.

The mother eagle is gentle with her youngsters. She broods them through the first week, then only at night and during bad weather for another three weeks. When the female approaches the tiny eaglets, she is very careful not to injure the youngsters with her deadly talons: She hobbles to them on limply folded toes.

26

The hunting methods of the golden eagle are more spectacular than those of the bald eagle. Diving at high speed, the bird comes suddenly upon its prey—usually a jackrabbit, marmot, or ground squirrel—and strikes with extended needle-sharp talons. It often hunts close above the ground and surprises its prey with a quick strike.

The golden eagle also attacks flying birds—such as grouse, ducks, and geese—and is able to pluck them out of the air. It will also feed on any dead fish, game, or farm animals it may find. On occasion, when there is a scarcity of its usual prey, the golden eagle will attack larger mammals—such as deer, antelope, bighorn sheep, and coyotes.

The bald eagle's favorite food is fish, but it can catch only those that feed or travel close to the surface.

As it nears its quarry, the eagle must carefully adjust its flight, taking in wind conditions and other factors.

Moving at high speed, it swings its feet forward, talons open, to make the grab. Its quarry—a fish head.

With the fish head in its talons, the eagle starts upward on its powerful wings.

Sometimes an eagle will grab a fish too

heavy for it to lift, and the eagle is in danger of drowning if it cannot get its talons loose. The bald eagle may rob an osprey, also called a fish hawk, which is an expert fisherman. It will also feed on dead or dying fish that have washed ashore.

When fish are not available, bald eagles feed on almost anything—including various seabirds, livestock killed on the road, dead deer, carrion of all kinds, and small rodents. At the Adak Naval Station in the Aleutian Islands, bald eagles have shown how adaptable they are by utilizing the station garbage dumps as a reliable food source. Areas where waterfowl gather in the winter provide a great deal of food for eagles. Mostly, however, the birds taken by eagles have been wounded by hunters and are either dead or too weak to survive.

After catching its prey, the eagle may hold it on the ground to eat or, if it is light enough, carry it to a perch above the ground. While holding the prey down with its feet, the bird plucks some of the fur or feathers, then tears off pieces of flesh with its powerful beak, and swallows them.

Parent eagles are kept busy finding food for themselves and their hungry eaglets. Adults may eat 1 to 2 pounds of food a day. Eaglets also eat a lot, grow fast, and at two weeks of age, they weigh eight to ten times as much as they did when hatched. In another two weeks, they may double this weight, and at about five weeks of age, they may weigh as much as thirty-two times their birth weight.

The golden eagle here is four to five weeks of age. Feathers have begun to appear. Note the size of this young bird as compared to the unhatched egg. Also, note the strange appearance of the eye. This is the nictitating membrane.

By the time they are a little over a month and a half old, eaglets will reach their maximum weight of around 8½ pounds. They may now consume 60 ounces of food a day, compared with the ¾ ounce a day they ate at hatching.

31

At three weeks or so, eaglets are strong enough to stand. They are now getting too large to be brooded, but their thicker, second covering of down makes them more resistant to the cold.

When they are six to eight weeks old, the young eagles have learned to feed themselves on food left by the parent birds and are strong enough to rip off pieces of the prey with their bills.

The golden eaglet above is making threatening gestures toward the photographer.

At eight to nine weeks of age, the golden eagle at right looks much like an adult.

If there are two eaglets, the older, and stronger, feeds first. The other gets what is left. Eagles and their young eat much of the prey that is not digestible—such as fur, feathers, or bones. Eventually, this material is regurgitated, and it is called a casting.

The broad expanse of the nest is an excellent playground and exercise field for the young birds. At first they merely scramble about, supported by wings and shanks. As they grow stronger, they prance around, clutch at nest sticks with their developing talons, and practice attacking prey by jumping about the nest, their talons extended. They exercise their wings by stretching and flapping. They begin to spend a lot of time preening their growing feathers. After these active periods, they rest and doze, their heads nodding on their breasts, their eyes closed.

Soon, this stretching and flapping becomes flight training, with a rhythmic wing beat and powerful sweeps that will raise the eaglet if its talons are not fastened tightly to the nest.

Before long, the eaglet attempts brief flights a few feet above the nest. It often does this facing a stiff wind, which helps it fly, but prevents it from leaving the nest.

At sixty-five to seventy days after birth, golden eaglets make their first flights. Just before this, the parent birds may not bring as much food to the nest as the youngsters are much too fat and flabby to fly. A few days without food will bring their weight down and their appetites up. The parents may then fly by the nest with meat in their talons so the hungry eaglets, now slim and trim, will want to fly after the food.

Bald eaglets leave the nest when they are seventy-two to seventy-five days old and may fly to one of the nearby perches the parent birds used during the nesting period. Despite their practice flying at the nest, the eaglets' first solo flights are often less than perfect and the landings awkward. Some eaglets may lose their balance and fall to the ground. Then it may be several days before they can work their way back to a higher perch. If an eaglet is unfortunate enough to fall into dense woods, it may never get out unless a parent bird can reach it with food.

After they first leave the nest, eaglets hang around the nest site for a month or more, depending on the parent birds for food while they develop their own hunting and flying skills.

Eagles do not migrate as much as do waterfowl and some other birds, but eagles that breed in northern areas will move south in the winter in search of food.

Despite the admiration expressed for eagles, especially the bald eagle, and the recognition of their many fine qualities, their only enemy is man. At one time, the Territory of Alaska paid a bounty for eagles killed, in the belief that their habit of feeding on fish was harmful to the Alaskan fishing industry. This has since been shown to be wrong. Most of the live fish caught by bald eagles are the less desirable species.

The destruction of feeding, nesting, and roosting sites has led to a decline in bald eagle populations. Also, disturbance by humans, especially during the early part of the nesting period, has seriously affected reproduction.

In recent years, bald eagle populations have been greatly endangered by chemical pollution. This has come from their eating of fish that inhabit polluted waters. Certain chemicals cause severe eggshell thinning, which results in frequent hatching failures. However, use of these chemicals has now been restricted, and the situation is improving.

Golden eagle populations have suffered from attacks by livestock producers, especially those raising sheep, who consider the bird a serious threat during lambing time.

Some ranchers who have been hard hit by hungry eagles have hired professional hunters. Operating from airplanes, these hunters have killed a great many golden eagles. In general, though, the eagle probably does more good than harm, because the small mammals that it hunts do a lot of damage to the range feed that livestock depends upon.

Power lines, attractive perches for eagles hunting in flat country, have caused the death by electrocution of many birds when their wings touched live wires on takeoffs or landings.

Here an employee of the Oregon Game Commission (right) assists a veterinarian as he examines a golden eagle that had apparently flown into a power line. Many injured eagles are cared for by game departments and authorized eagle rehabilitation centers. If they recover, the eagles are permitted to go free. Otherwise they are turned over to zoos where they are cared for and displayed.

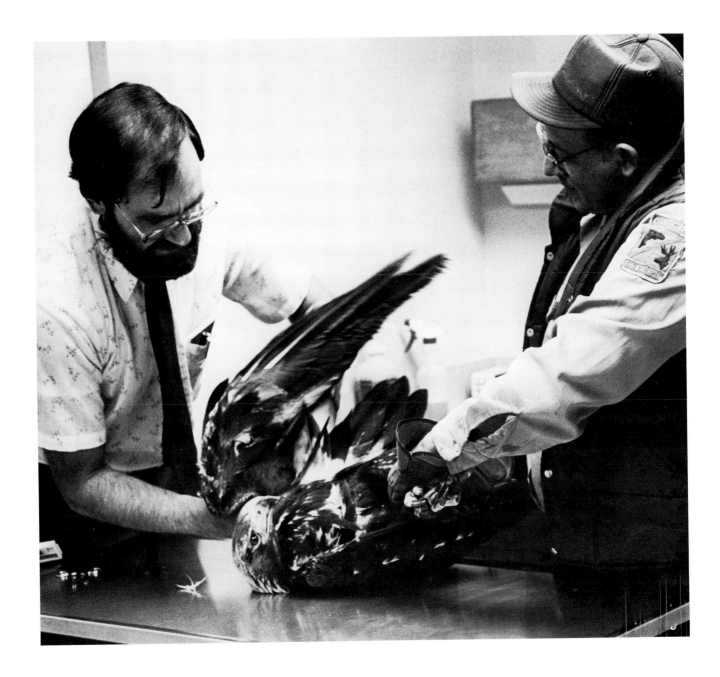

From the earliest times, there have been persistent legends of eagles carrying off small children, or lambs, or other small animals. However, recent studies on captive birds indicate that these are just stories. An eagle does not fly easily with more than 2½ pounds attached to its feet. From the ground, and with the help of a strong wind, an eagle can lift and carry about 8 pounds. Under the most favorable circumstances, an eagle might carry off an animal about its own weight—9 to 12 pounds.

Thoughtless hunters shoot eagles, both bald and golden, for no reason at all. Many zoos have cared for wounded eagles that have been rescued. Sometimes these birds recover completely and are released in the wilds. Mostly, however, they are unable to care for themselves and must remain in zoos.

Many things are now being done to protect eagles, hawks, and owls. In 1940, laws were passed making it unlawful to kill, possess, sell, or trade any live or dead bald eagle, or any part of one—including feathers, eggs, and nests. In 1943, Alaska discontinued paying bounties 41 for eagles. In 1963, the golden eagle was given much the same protection as the bald eagle. Since 1966, eagle nesting sites in all national wildlife refuges have been given protection.

The 1978 Endangered Species Act listed the bald eagle as endangered in forty-three of the lower forty-eight states and threatened in the other five—Oregon, Washington, Michigan, Minnesota, and Wisconsin. The bald and the golden eagle are also protected under the Bald Eagle Protection Act and, along with other migratory birds, under the Migratory Bird

42

Treaty Act. As of 1982, it has been illegal to bother any eagle in any way.

In addition to the protection being given by federal, state, and local law enforcement agencies, a great deal of scientific study is being devoted to eagles to ensure their future well-being. For release in the wild, some eagles are being hatched from the eggs of captive birds. Also, organizations—such as the National Audubon Society, the National Wildlife Federation, the Nature Conservancy, and some universities—are contributing in various ways to this cause.

The following photographs show the activities of a team from the Oregon Cooperative Wildlife Research Unit, Department of Fisheries and Wildlife, Oregon State University, banding young bald eagles in south central Oregon.

A climber approaches a massive eagle nest situated 150 feet aboveground in an evergreen tree overlooking Klamath Lake. These climbs are arduous and dangerous, but climbers are experienced and use safety ropes. Supplies the climber needs when he gets into the nest are carried in his backpack. Often, the most difficult part of the climb is getting into the nest. Great care is exercised so as not to unduly frighten the young birds.

A young bald eagle threatens the nest intruder.

In a perching tree a hundred yards away, the female waits, watches, and screeches her objections.

46

At intervals, one of the parent birds
flies over the tree. Adults rarely, if ever,
attack the bird banders.

The team member at the nest carefully captures one of the young birds, puts a hood over its head, a sack over its sharp and dangerous claws, and wraps it in a soft cloth so it cannot flap and hurt its wings. The bird is then placed in a large sack and lowered gently to the team members on the ground. After this bird is processed, it will be returned, and its nest mate will receive the same treatment.

When the young bird is removed from the sack, it looks like the one at right.

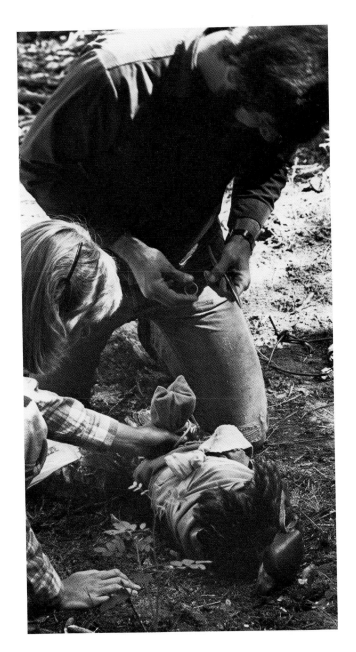

A numbered metal tag is attached to a leg, for future identification of the bird. When hooded and wrapped, the young bird remains docile.

For a special study being conducted on eagles all over the country, a blood sample is carefully and painlessly taken from the bird's wing.

Unwrapped for further examination, the young eagle above, now as large as an adult, tries its wings.

By now the young bird has become accustomed to being handled, and at right it remains calm.

As a result of the measures being taken, the recent decline of eagle populations may have come to a halt. In fact, populations are on the increase. A midwinter survey in early 1982 indicated 13,904 bald eagles in the forty-eight contiguous states, an increase of 5 percent over 1980. The bald eagle in Alaska has never been seriously threatened, and with the elimination of Alaska's bounty system, the population, currently estimated at around 35,000, should increase. Another 40,000 to 50,000 bald eagles remain in Canada. The wintering population of golden eagles in the lower forty-eight states rises as the birds migrate from Canada and Alaska. The population is estimated at 40,000 to 50,000 birds and, in areas not subject to human disturbance, remains about the same from year to year.

As a symbol of our country, the bald eagle was well chosen. Some people think the golden eagle was equally or, possibly, more suitable. Both are noble birds that deserve better treatment than we have given them in the past. Fortunately, those who care about eagles are now supporting their legal protection, and the future should be brighter for these noble birds.

INDEX

Adak Naval Station, 30
Alaska, 24, 37, 52
Aleutian Islands, 30
American eagle, *see* bald eagle
Armstrong, Neil A., 19

bald eagle (American eagle;
    Haliaeetus leucocephalus):
  adaptability of, 30
  description of, 1, 4
  eaglets of, 25–26, 37
  fishing methods of, 29
  flight of, 7, 37
  hunting methods of, 7, 11,
    29
  incubation period of, 24–25
  naming of, 1

bald eagle, *continued*
  as national symbol, 18, 52
  nests of, 21–24
  populations of, 52
  prey of, 30
  sound of, 13
Bald Eagle Protection Act, 42
bathing, 8
beaks, 1, 2, 12
Boy Scouts of America, 18
breeding season, 22

Canada, 52
commercial products, 19

Department of Fisheries and
  Wildlife, 44

Eagle (lunar module), 19
eagle population, endangerment
  of, 37–42, 50–52
  bounty payments and, 37,
    41–42
  by chemical pollution, 38
  eagle population rise and, 52
  by hunters, 41
  laws and, 41–42
  by livestock producers, 38
  by power lines, 38
  scientific study of, 42–49
eagles:
  banding of, 44–49
  eating habits of, 30
  egg laying of, 24
  hearing of, 11

eagles, *continued*
    hunting by, 11
    life span of, 1
    mating of, 22
    migration of, 37
    nesting sites of, 21
    as symbol, 14–21, 52
    vision of, 5
    see also bald eagle; golden
        eagle
Eagle Scouts, 18
eaglets:
    description of, 25
    feeding of, 26
    incubation of, 24
    mother eagle's care for, 26
    relationships among, 26, 34
    weight of, 25, 30, 31
egg laying, 24
Endangered Species Act, 42
eyelids, 9

falconry, 14
feathers, 3, 4, 17
    of eaglets, 25
    molting of, 9

feathers, *continued*
    preening of, 8
feet, 1, 2, 11

golden eagle *(Aquila
        chrysaëtos)*:
    description of, 1, 3
    eaglets of, 25–26, 34
    flight of, 5, 34
    hunting methods of, 5, 11, 27
    incubation period of, 24
    nests of, 21–24
    prey of, 27
    regional habitats of, 24
    sound of, 13
Great Seal, U.S., 17

Indians, American, 17
Interior Department, U.S., 17

Klamath Lake, 44

Migratory Bird Treaty Act,
    42
molting, 9
money, eagle's image on, 17

National Audubon Society, 42
National Wildlife Federation,
    42
Nature Conservancy, 42
nests, 21–24
    construction of, 22
    eaglet play and exercise in,
        34
    materials for, 22
    sites of, 21, 24
    size of, 23
nictitating membrane, 9, 30

Old Stone Age, 14
Oregon Cooperative Wildlife
    Research Unit, 44
Oregon Game Commission, 38
Oregon State University, 44

postage stamps, 18

state seals, 18

talons, 2, 11

wingspan, 1

DISCARD